*Bangers and Mash are two naughty chimps who live with Mum, Dad and Gran at number 3 Tree Street, Chimpton. You can read about their amazing adventures in the books in this series.*

British Library Cataloguing in Publication Data
Groves, Paul
  Eggs is eggs
  I. Title    II. McLachlan, Edward, *1940–*    III. Series
  823′.914 [J]
  ISBN 0-7214-1221-1

First edition

Published by Ladybird Books Ltd  Loughborough  Leicestershire  UK
Ladybird Books Inc  Auburn  Maine 04210  USA
© LADYBIRD BOOKS LTD MCMLXXXIX
© LONGMAN GROUP UK LTD/FILMFAIR LTD MCMLXXXIX

Printed in England

# Bangers & Mash
## Eggs is eggs

*by* Paul Groves
*illustrations by* Edward McLachlan

Ladybird Books

Far, far away, further than you
have ever been on your holidays —
there is an island.

The island is covered in trees.
Bright coloured birds nest in the
trees. But as well as birds' nests
there are also some houses.

They look like ordinary, nice houses, but they are built up in the trees – right off the ground.

Those houses are in Chimpton – a town of chimpanzees. And in Chimpton, at number 3 Tree Street, live Bangers and Mash with Mum, Dad and Gran.

Bangers doesn't look much like a sausage. He looks more like a cheeky chimpanzee.

Mash doesn't look like a plate of squashed up potato either. He looks like another cheeky chimp.

Mum has plenty on her plate
looking after the two of them.

Bangers is a bit bigger than Mash.
He has a B on his tie.

Mash has an M on his tee shirt.
The letters stand for Bangers and
Mash, but they could be for 'Bother'
and 'Mess' the tricks those chimps
get up to.

One morning at number 3 there was a typical scene.

Mum was dusting. Dad was in the vegetable garden planting some carrot seeds. Gran was having a nap in her chair on the lawn. And Bangers and Mash were playing football. But they needed a goal.

A tree stump made one goal post. Gran in her chair made the other post.

A creeper made a crossbar and a friendly bird, perched on Gran's head, held it at just the right height.

So Bangers and Mash began their football practice.

Mash went in goal and Bangers fired in a fierce shot. Mash dived for the ball and just got his finger tips to it.

The ball hit the 'post' and went in off it.

Poor Gran, she had scored an own goal as she fell over backwards.

Mum was not very pleased. And
neither was Gran.

"Go away and play somewhere
else, you chimps," said Mum.
"Gran doesn't want to play
with you. She needs her rest."

So Bangers and Mash
went swinging off
through the
trees.

They swung all the way to the pond. It was very quiet there. (Or it was till Bangers and Mash arrived.)

The first thing they saw was the Duck, quacking along through the reeds. She was going to her nest to do a spot of hatching. She had six eggs, and she was expecting her ducklings to come out of their shells at any moment. She squatted down on the eggs.

Bangers and Mash were squatting too in the reeds as they crept towards the nest to get a better view. But the Duck saw them coming. She knew all about Bangers and Mash. They meant trouble with a big 'T'.

The eggs would have to wait for a moment.

As Bangers and Mash crept
towards the nest, the Duck stuck
out her head and gave a warning
squawk. Bangers and Mash froze.
Then the Duck took off into the
air and Bangers and Mash took off
as well. But the dive-bombing duck
zoomed after them. She was on the
warpath.

The Duck knew what she was doing.
She drove Bangers and Mash
towards the muddy pond.

*Splosh! Squelch! Ooze!*

Bangers and Mash found themselves
taking a mud bath. They had
been given a right
*ducking!*

Mum was not at all pleased. They had to change all their clothes. She told them to keep away from the pond. But they were very curious and they could not resist going back.

All was quiet again down by the reeds. The Duck had left her nest to feed in the pond.

Suddenly, one of the
eggs cracked and
split wide open.
Out of the shell
stepped a fluffy yellow duckling.

Then the other five eggs also
cracked and split open. Five more
fluffy yellow ducklings
stepped out of
their shells.

Bangers and Mash were thrilled.
It was the first time they had
seen eggs hatching. They
watched, fascinated.

The ducklings were going
'Cheep! Cheep!'
But weren't they
*dear*.

Bangers and
Mash wanted
to tell Mum,
Dad and Gran
all about the
ducklings.

The sun was still shining, but
Bangers and Mash were tucked up
in bed.

Why were they in bed?

Did they have colds after the
ducking?

Had they got spots?

Was hatching catching?

But Bangers left a trail of broken eggs which Dad *eggs-amined*.

"What's this?" cried Dad, following the eggy footprints. They led straight to his armchair. It was covered in yolks and shells. Dad didn't see the funny side. In fact, he *eggs-ploded*!

Just then Mum, Dad and Gran arrived back home from the Chimpermarket.

"I left six eggs on this table for tea," said Mum looking at the empty plate as they went into the kitchen.

Bangers and Mash groaned. They tried to creep out without being seen.

Then he sat on the eggs and Mash
pressed the button of the camera.

There was a big flash!

There was also a big *Splosh!
Squelch! Ooze!*

The shells had cracked. But there
weren't any ducklings. Only
scrambled egg all over Dad's chair.

Bangers was going to sit on the eggs to hatch them like the Duck.

Mash went upstairs to get his camera. They wanted some pictures of the ducklings coming out of their shells.

Mash pointed the camera at Bangers. "Say 'Cheese'," he said. Bangers gave a big smile.

They picked them up and carried them into the lounge. Mash tripped in the doorway but just managed to stop his eggs falling.

There in the corner stood a big armchair. It was Dad's chair. They put the eggs carefully on a cushion.

Bangers and Mash were alone in the house.

But there on the kitchen table were six eggs for tea. Two for Dad and one each for Mum, Gran and Bangers and Mash.

Bangers looked at the eggs.

Mash looked at the eggs.

They raced back through the trees
to number 3 Tree Street.

There was no one on the lawn.
Gran had finished her nap.

There was no one in the garden.
Dad had finished his planting.

There was no one in the house.
Mum had finished the dusting.

Dad had taken Mum and Gran to
the Chimpermarket in the car.

No, Dad was so cross that he put Bangers and Mash to bed without any tea. Now they had to lie there with their stomachs rumbling.

It had been an *eggs-citing* day until now. Those chimps had certainly learned that *eggs is eggs*.